Young Learner's

Jungle Tales

The Lazy Hare

The Crab and the Crane

The Lazy Hare

A long time ago scorching winds blew across the plains of Africa. The sun shone down mercilessly. The grass was reduced to a crisp and all the watering holes dried up.

The animals were very worried. The King Lion called an urgent meeting. All the forest animals—elephant, zebra, giraffe, hyena, monkey, hippopotamus, fox and deer—gathered together. Only the lazy hare did not show up. As usual, he was sleeping in his burrow.

King Lion said, "The heat is blistering and there is still no sign of rain. What are we going to do?"

Everyone looked at the wise elephant for a solution. She thought deeply and then said, “I remember the time when I was a calf. There were no rains and it had become very hot. There was a wildfire and my mother took us towards North where a mighty river flows which never dries out. We all should go there without any delay.”

A horrified murmur ran through the group. Would they have to leave their homes and go to a new land? Everyone began talking at once and there was a lot of confusion. King Lion roared, “Quiet, everyone! The elephant is right. We must leave for the river before night falls. We shall return when it rains.”

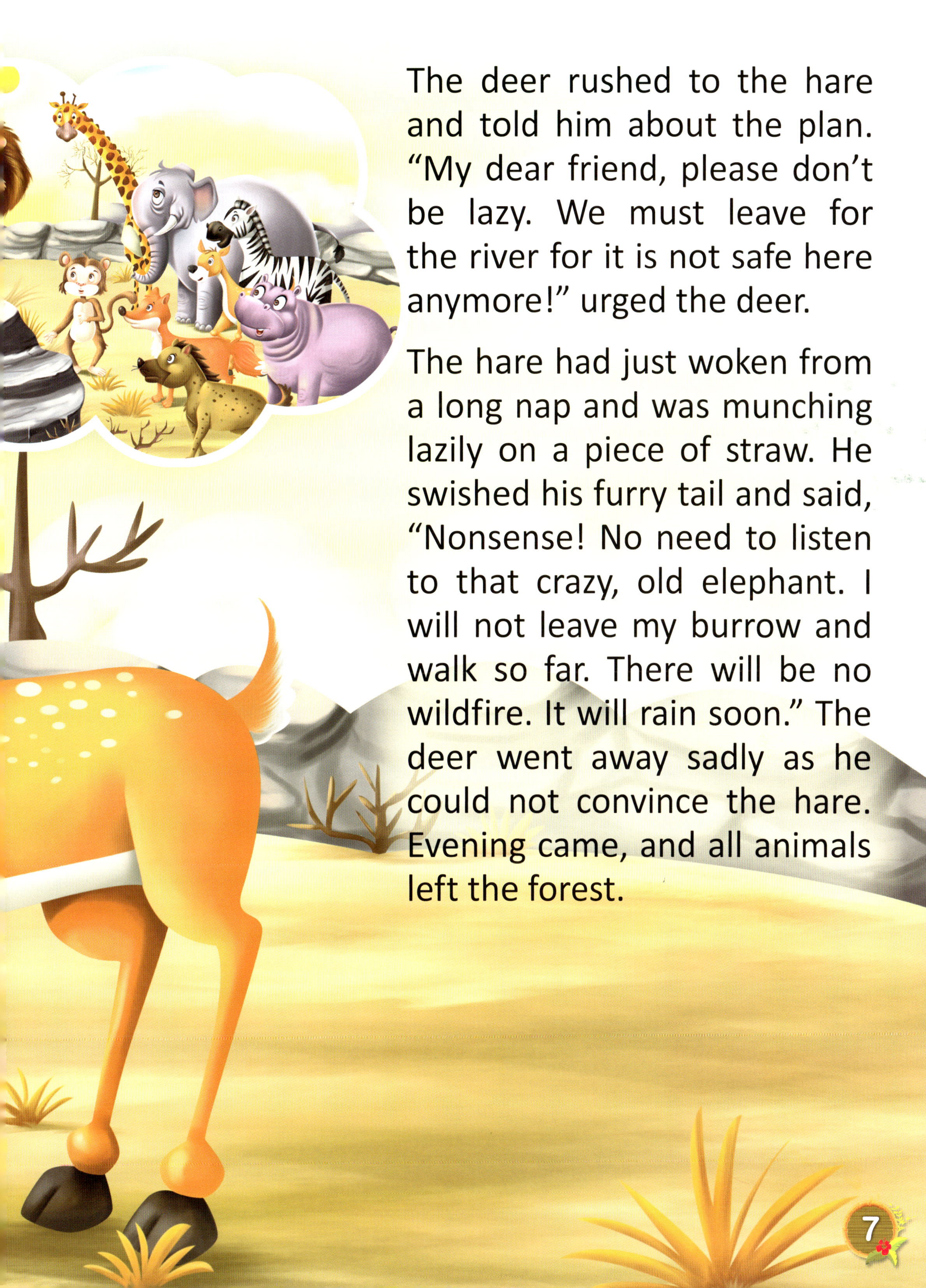

The deer rushed to the hare and told him about the plan. "My dear friend, please don't be lazy. We must leave for the river for it is not safe here anymore!" urged the deer.

The hare had just woken from a long nap and was munching lazily on a piece of straw. He swished his furry tail and said, "Nonsense! No need to listen to that crazy, old elephant. I will not leave my burrow and walk so far. There will be no wildfire. It will rain soon." The deer went away sadly as he could not convince the hare. Evening came, and all animals left the forest.

Next afternoon, the hare was woken up by a crackling sound. Grey smoke filled his burrow and he could barely breathe. "Wildfire!" he cried out, and ran out of his hole. He was horrified to see flames everywhere. His tail caught fire. Somehow he managed to put out the fire. He quickly climbed a rocky outcrop and cowered in fear and pain. He would survive but his fluffy tail was gone. He realised his mistake and said to himself, "I should have listened to the deer and left with everyone else. I will never be lazy again."

The Crab and the Crane

Once upon a time, there was a cunning old crane. One day, he thought of a clever plan to catch fish. He just stood in the water and pretended to look sad.

A fish asked the crane, “Why are you not trying to catch us today?” The crane replied, “I am worried about your safety. A group of fishermen will soon arrive at the pond. They will catch you all in their fishing nets.”

The fishes began crying, “We don’t want to die.”

The crane replied, “Don’t worry, I shall shift all of you to a stream far away from here. You will be safe there.”

The foolish fish were grateful to the crane. They requested him to take them to the stream immediately.

The crane agreed and took away the first fish in his beak. As soon as the pond was out of sight he gobbled up the fish. Then he returned for another fish. It met with the same fate as the first one. Thus, one by one the crane carried away many fishes and had a great feast. This went on for a few days.

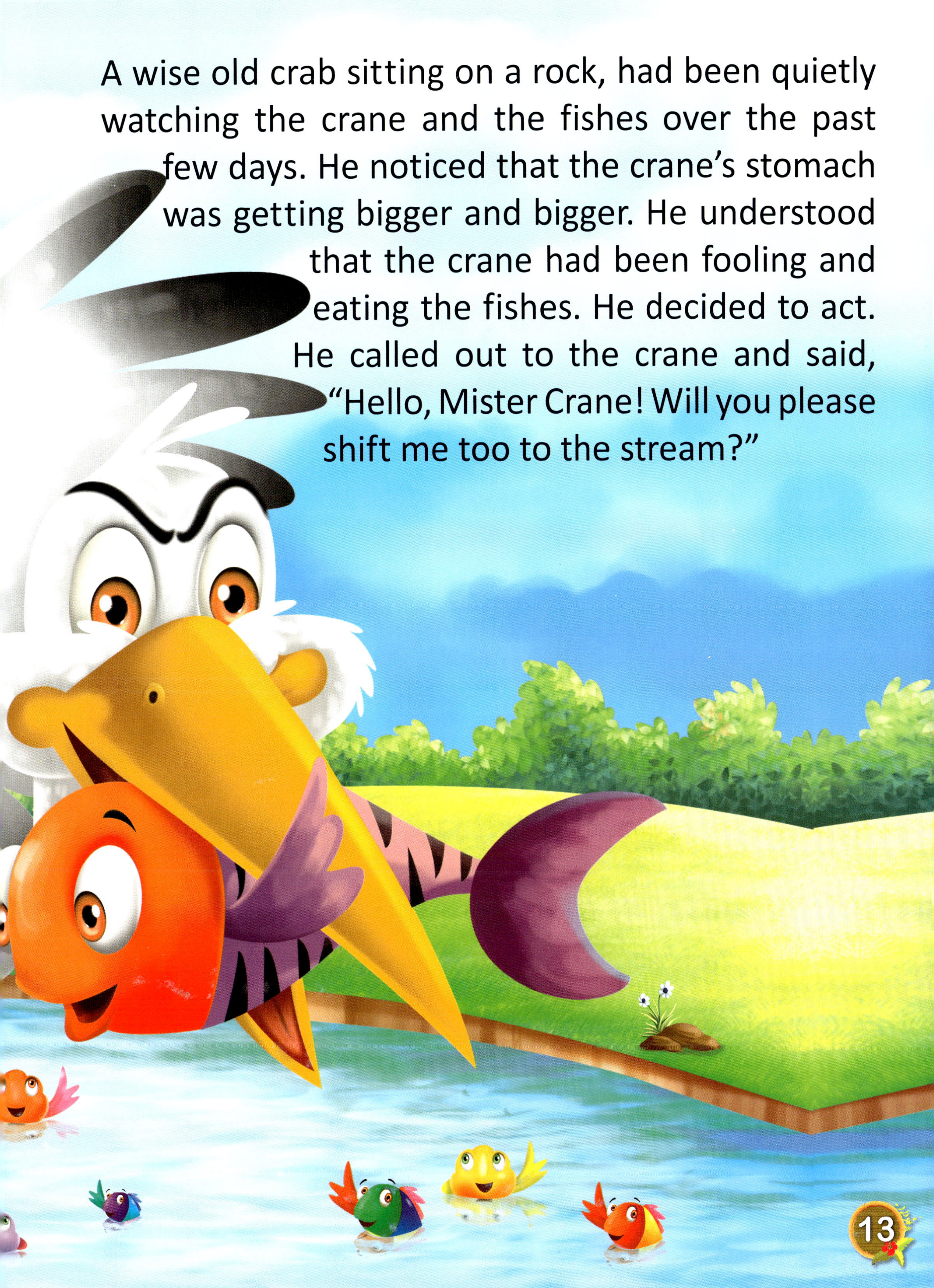

A wise old crab sitting on a rock, had been quietly watching the crane and the fishes over the past few days. He noticed that the crane's stomach was getting bigger and bigger. He understood that the crane had been fooling and eating the fishes. He decided to act. He called out to the crane and said, "Hello, Mister Crane! Will you please shift me too to the stream?"

The crane was delighted. His mouth watered at the thought of eating the crab. He replied, “Of course! I will shift you too.” He tried to pick up the crab with his beak but the crab was too big.

“Don’t worry, Mister Crane. I will sit on your back and then you can fly me to the stream,” said the crab. The crane agreed and the crab climbed onto the crane’s back. As they flew over a grassland, the crab’s suspicions were confirmed. There were fish bones lying everywhere.

“It is now or never!” decided the crab. He opened his claws wide and snapped them close around the crane’s neck with all his might. That was the end of the cunning crane. The crab returned to the pond and told the remaining fishes about the evil plan of the crane. They realised their foolishness and thanked the wise crab for saving their lives.